A PARRAGON BOOK
Published by Parragon Book Service Ltd, Unit 13-17 Avonbridge Trading Estate,
Atlantic Road, Avonmouth, Bristol BS11 9QD
Produced by The Templar Company plc, Pippbrook Mill,
London Road, Dorking, Surrey RH4 1JE
Copyright © 1995 Parragon Book Service Limited
All rights reserved
Printed and bound in Italy
ISBN 0-75250-867-9

PICTURE TALES

The Ugly Duckling

Illustrated by Tom Pepperday

∥ ·PARRAGON· ∥

It was summer and the countryside looked beautiful. Down by the 🏞 a 🦆 had made her 🪺, and was now sitting proudly on six lovely 🥚. Five 🥚 were white,

but the sixth was large and grey. At last the cracked and five fluffy yellow  appeared. But when the sixth hatched, a large, ugly, grey came out. Mother Duck

was disappointed, but she took the ugly duckling to the 🏞️ with the other 🐥🐥, and was pleased to find he was a strong swimmer. She told them to watch out for the 🐱 .

But it was the other 🦆🦆, not the 🐱, that hurt the 🐥. They laughed when they saw the 🐥, and pecked at him. Even the 👧 who fed them pushed him aside with her 👟.

His mother tried to protect him, but it was no use. So the decided to run away. He went to the marsh where the wild lived, and nestled there in the . Some came by and

wanted to make friends, but just then a 🧍 with a big 🔫 came along and scared the 🦆🦆 away.

The 🐤 hid in the 🌾 feeling very scared and lonely.

A big 🐕 appeared, growling and baring his 🦷, but he went away again. "I'm even too ugly for the 🐕 to touch," thought the 🦆. When it was dark he ran till he reached a 🏠,

where an old 🧓 , a 🐔 and a 🐈 lived. The 🐔 and 🐈 ruled the 🏠 , but because the 🐤 could not lay 🥚 , or hunt 🐁 , they were not interested in him.

The 🦆 returned to the 🏞 and stayed there alone, through autumn, when the 🌳 turned golden, and then through the harsh cold winter. ❄ came and the 🏞 froze.

But at last spring came, and the ☀ shone again. By now the 🦢 had grown much larger, and when he flapped his 🪽 he rose up into the air, above the 🌳 and 🏠.

He landed smoothly on a 🏞, and saw three 🦢 floating towards him. He looked down in shame, thinking how ugly he must look, and was amazed to see his own reflection.

He was no longer an , but a beautiful ! He soon made friends with the other  and the village who fed him every day. His was filled with happiness at last!